# MINERS

### Volume 9

### Tales of the Wild West Series

## Rick Steber

## Illustrations by Don Gray

NOTE
MINERS is the ninth book in the
Tales of the Wild West series.

MINERS
Volume 9
Tales of the Wild West series

**Bonanza Publishing**
Box 204
Prineville, Oregon 97754

# Tales of the Wild West

# INTRODUCTION

James Marshall, who was building a sawmill for John Sutter on the American River in the Sierra Nevada foothills, turned water from the millpond into the tailrace and saw a glimmer in the clear water. He bent and picked up a yellow rock about the size of a dime. He saw more shiny stones and gathered these, too.

On January 23, 1848 John Sutter wrote in his diary that Marshall, "soaked to the skin and dripping water," came bursting into his office "informing me he had something of utmost importance to tell me in private."

Word of the gold discovery at Sutter's mill soon leaked out and 80,000 miners rushed to California hoping to claim a share of the big strike. They dug gold from the hills and streambeds and when the easy-pickings played out they moved on to the eastern slopes of the Sierra Nevada and into the Rocky Mountains. Other disgruntled miners moved to the Northwest, and finally the lure of gold drove prospectors to the Alaskan frontier.

The typical miner was a young man who dressed in a slouch hat, red long johns and trousers tucked into high-topped boots. He packed a shovel, pick and gold pan. When his dream of easy riches eventually died, as it almost always did, the young man stayed in the West and became a farmer, stockman, tradesman or professional. If married, he sent for his wife and children and if single, he married a daughter of a pioneer family.

The lasting effect of the gold rush was not so much measured in the individual accumulation of wealth, but in the simple fact that thousands of miners came west, and rather than returning home, stayed and helped to settle the West.

# THE MEDICINE MAN

"Word of the big gold strike at Sutter's mill proved to be a temptation for a man to leave his homestead and family and give prospecting a try," stated Drew Hodges, an Oregon pioneer. "It was too big of a temptation for me. In the company of 10 other homesteaders, including my brother Cal and a Calapooia Indian we hired to serve as guide, we started south the summer of 18 and 49.

"Our journey was uneventful until we reached the Rogue River. The Indians here were on the warpath and a large band of renegades were congregated on the south bank. They made it very evident, if we were to attempt a crossing, they would kill us.

"Some of my companions tried to loft a few potshots across the water but the Indians made sure they remained beyond rifle range. Each time a shot was fired, the medicine man ran to the water's edge and acted like he was catching the bullet in his teeth.

"My brother Cal was in possession of a Kentucky long rifle which had belonged to our father. In fact, it was named in his honor, 'Old Jim'. I told Cal, 'Let's see what 'Old Jim' can do.' He handed me the rifle.

"I drew a bead on the medicine man, who was still taunting us, gathered a deep breath, held it and pulled the trigger. A full three counts later the medicine man grabbed at his chest and fell over backwards. I turned to Cal, told him, 'He didn't catch it with his teeth but, by God, he caught her.'

"The Indians scattered. We drove our horses into the water and continued on toward California and the gold."

# THE DREAM

Jim McGarvey was an Easterner who was attracted to California by the fantastic stories he heard about gold nuggets lying around for the taking. Upon his arrival in the West he discovered the stories had been true, but only for the first lucky few.

For Jim the dreams of instant wealth died hard. He drifted north to the Klamath Mountains and continued to fervently believe that, with the next shovel of gravel, he was going to discover the mother lode.

Jim never married. He devoted his entire existence to the fruitless search for gold. One of his mining partners, Alex Watts, recalled, "No doubt about it, Jim was an odd duck. There came a day when his mind just snapped and he began to rant and rave.

"I caught him up on the hill destroying the pipeline to our sluice and when I tried to stop him he pulled his knife and came at me. He sliced me across the chest. I've still got the scar to prove it.

"From all those years spent moving gravel he was as strong as a bear, but somehow I managed to subdue him. I tied him with a rope, sent word to the sheriff and he came and took him away."

The dreams of the 66-year-old miner had become insane delusions and Jim McGarvey spent the remainder of his days confined at the State of Oregon Mental Hospital.

# JUMPING OFF

"This break in the weather gives us a chance to jump off early. We'll get to the digging first and stake our claims," a miner told his partners.

"Pretty risky. If another storm blows in we'll be trapped in the mountains. Better think it over," stated another. But he was outvoted and it was decided the six men, with three-day's rations, would head out at first light the following morning.

The six prospectors encountered snow on the pass and the going was slow. A fierce blizzard overtook them and they were forced to make camp where they remained until, out of food and with the storm still howling around them, they voted to turn back.

On the sixth day of their ordeal they came across a woodpecker. One of the men killed it and made soup. The seventh day they stripped bark off willow trees and ate that. Suddenly one of the miners, a Frenchman, exclaimed, "I know where we are. The main camp is just over that ridge. The fellows there have a big fire goin'. Meat's cookin'. Can't ya smell it? Ain't your mouth just a waterin'? Think how good it'll taste. Come on, boys. Follow me."

The Frenchman broke trail and led the others to the camp where a spontaneous celebration erupted. The Frenchman was handed a jug of whiskey. He took a long drink. But in his weakened condition the alcohol proved fatal. It stopped his heart and killed him.

# INDIAN GOLD

The old Indian woman, who the miners called Dolly, claimed she was puzzled when the white men first came to the Klamath River country because they spent all their time digging in the gravel bars searching for gold. She reasoned that gold was not something that could be eaten, or wrapped about a person's shoulders to keep out the cold, and she was even more bewildered when the white men said gold was worth money. She had no concept of money.

What caught Dolly's eye was not gold but the possessions brought by the miners. She desired their trinkets, red cloth and mirrors that flashed in the sun. She wanted a brass kettle to hang over the fire and keep water hot. She wanted her husband to have iron so he could fashion it into a knife.

Dolly claimed, "Indian never dig gold. Let white man dig gold. Indian watch white man. When white man not looking, steal from white man.

"One time me watch white man. See him dig hole. See him bury tin can. Think him bury gold. Wait for him leave. Dig up tin can. Find green paper. Me not want green paper. Throw can, throw green paper, in river."

Her story concluded, Dolly threw back her head and laughed. And when she stopped laughing she explained it was not until much later she discovered, "To white man green paper just like gold."

5

# JACKSONVILLE

Luckless miners who failed to strike it rich in California drifted north and discovered placer gold on Jackson Creek in southern Oregon.

The town of Jacksonville quickly became a boomtown. It was said that in the early days gold was found almost everywhere. To prove the point, miners told about the time two men who were incarcerated in the town jail tried to tunnel out. In the process they hit a pocket of placer gold and thereafter, even though they had completed their sentences, they were reluctant to leave. It was estimated that between 1853 and 1880 more than $31 million worth of gold was removed from the claims along Jackson Creek.

The heyday of Jacksonville was marked by a visit from President Rutherford B. Hayes. He attended a gala ball held in his honor and, after shaking hands with every respectable Republican in town, he retired to the United States Hotel, said to be the finest accommodations between Portland and San Francisco.

In the morning Madame Holt, the proprietor of the hotel and a colorful local celebrity, handed an aide of President Hayes a bill. The aide took one look at the charge of $100 for a night's lodging and declared, "Madame, perhaps there is a misunderstanding—we do not wish to purchase your hotel."

Madame Holt prevailed and the bill was paid. But years later, when President Hayes wrote his memoirs, he got even, writing of his stay in Jacksonville, "I did not mind spending the evening in town with local supporters of my political party. But I did strenuously object to spending the remainder of the night in the United States Hotel with the entire Democratic Party—the army of bedbugs which joined me in the Presidential Suite."

# THE SEARCH

George Jackson came west looking to strike it rich in the gold fields but after several years he gave up and headed for home. On the way he happened across a hot mineral spring and on January 6, 1859 he wrote in his diary, "Beautiful mountain sheep all grazing about the springs where the warm vapors have melted the snow and left the grass for them to nibble at." He shot one of the sheep and fixed himself dinner. Heartened by the meal he decided to spend one more day looking for gold.

In the morning he located a promising-looking sandbar and collected more than an ounce of gold. He wrote in his diary, "After a good supper of meat—bread and coffee all gone—went to bed and dreamed of riches galore in that bar. If only I had a pick and shovel I could dig out a sack full of the yellow stuff."

George staked a claim and, since he could do little work until spring thaw, he continued on to Denver where he mentioned his good fortune to only one man, a trusted friend who according to George, was "as tight lipped as a Number 4 beaver trap."

In spite of that, word leaked out and a gold rush ensued. George was talked into selling his claim for a modest sum. But his discovery yielded more than $100 million worth of gold.

# BIG BEN

Big Ben was famous around the mining camps of the West for his exploits of strength. One time a traveling circus came to camp and a prize was offered to anyone who could defeat what was advertised as the "World Champion Wrestling Bear." Big Ben accepted the challenge. He stepped inside the cage and when the bear raised onto its hind legs Big Ben grabbed the bear, and to the wild cheers of the miners, flipped the bear on it's back and pinned it.

Big Ben finally met his match the night he brought a jug of his special home-made brew to the saloon. He offered the jug to a friend and this man took a tentative sip and promptly spit it out, exclaiming, "That's horrible! This stuff would eat a hole through boiler plate."

Big Ben reclaimed his jug, turned to address the room and told the miners, "Boys, you all know I'm the strongest man in these here parts. And I say I'm man enough to drink a whole jug of my sweet raisin brew."

With that he lifted the jug to his lips, threw back his head and gulped down the entire contents of the jug. An eyewitness described what happened next. "Well, Big Ben stood there like a statue and then all of a sudden his eyes rolled back in his head and he keeled over, out cold."

The following morning Big Ben returned to the saloon and was asked about his performance the night before. He shrugged his massive shoulders and claimed, "Don't remember nothin'." He rubbed his head and in a reserved voice remarked, "In the future I ain't agonna put in ... quite ... so many raisins."

# FRIENDSHIP

A group of Oregon men were returning home from the rich California diggings when 19-year-old George Hunt came down with mountain fever. Around the campfire that evening the men discussed what they should do. It was obvious George was too sick to travel and some of the men were for leaving him. It was suggested that, since either the fever or Indians would get the boy, the others should divide up his poke. But two men, Sappington and Bush, refused to leave a friend on the trail and volunteered to stay with the boy.

They kept the fire going all that day and tried to make the boy as comfortable as possible. As evening was coming on a war party of Indians gathered for an attack and Sappington told Bush, "If we don't use the night to get away the Indians will kill us sure as heck."

"Do we leave him?" Bush nodded toward George.

"I've got an idea," said Sappington. "We'll make a travois out of two poles and a blanket, just like the Indians do. We'll drag him."

The two men pulled the travois over the rugged Siskiyou Mountains and finally reached the Willamette Valley where they located George Hunt's father. They gave the man his son, who was recovering from mountain fever, as well as handing over a poke of gold dust worth more than $4,000.

# CRAZY BOB

Bob Womack was working on a ranch in Colorado when he found an interesting rock in Cripple Creek (named because cattle were sometimes crippled in the boulder-strewn creek bed). The rock was dull gray, about the size of a man's fist and very heavy. Bob had the rock assayed and it proved to be very rich ore, containing almost 20 ounces of gold to the ton.

Bob guessed his specimen was float rock that had washed downstream and began searching for the mother lode. Travelers reported seeing a man roaming the creek and hillsides and often times he had a whiskey jug in hand. They would laugh and tell, "He'd drink a while and shovel a while." Over the course of a dozen years Bob dug hundreds of holes and earned the nickname, "Crazy Bob."

In 1890 the search paid off. Crazy Bob filed a claim in Poverty Gulch, near where he had found the original, gold-laden rock. He began sinking a shaft into the side of the hill and named his mine the El Paso.

But Crazy Bob, on a wild drinking spree, parted with title to the El Paso for $300. The claim was developed, earned more than $3 million dollars and set off a boom that attracted more than 20,000 miners. When Crazy Bob died in 1909 he did not have a penny to his name.

# INDIANS

After gold was discovered in Eastern Oregon thousands of prospectors rushed in. The Indians resisted this invasion, taking potshots at the miners while they worked and driving off their stock at every opportunity.

To protect the miners the 1st Cavalry of Oregon Volunteers, under the command of Lt. James Waymire, was dispatched from Fort Dalles. They set camp near the diggings at Canyon City and waited for the Indians' next move. The response came quickly. The Indians waylaid a pack outfit and stole the supplies and animals.

Lt. Waymire left a small detachment to guard the main camp while he led the remaining volunteers into battle. They followed the Indians over the mountains and finally overtook them near Harney Lake. But the Indians forced the volunteers to retreat and they continued their withdrawal all the way to Canyon City.

Upon reaching their main camp the volunteers discovered the Indians had already been there and had driven off all the remounts and attacked Canyon City where two miners were killed.

Reinforcements were sent in. This time they were able to drive the Indians away. They kept them on the run and eventually forced the various tribes of eastern Oregon to sign treaties and live on reservations.

# THE MINT

A few months after gold was discovered in the Rocky Mountains three Denver men, brothers Austin and Milton Clark, and E.E. Gruber opened a bank. They traded hard currency for gold dust, shipping the dust east for minting.

"We're paying a 5% express charge to the shippers, plus another 5% for insurance. On top of that, it takes three months to get back the coins. We can't run a business like that," reasoned Austin Clark. In addition to working as a banker, Austin was also an attorney. He informed his partners, "There are no laws forbidding private minting, as long as the coin is full-weight."

The partners purchased coining equipment and the July 25, 1860 edition of the *Rocky Mountain News* reported, "The little engine that drives the machinery was fired up, belts adjusted and between three and four o'clock 'mint drops', of the value of $10 each, began dropping into a tin pail with the most musical chink."

The gold dust of the region's mining camps was stamped "Pikes Peak Gold." During the three years of its operation the Denver mint coined nearly $600,000 and established a world-wide reputation for the quality of the region's gold. The mint operated until the federal government, fearing competition, purchased it.

# CAVE-IN

Frank Crampton, described what it was like being trapped underground in a cave-in at Goldfield, Nevada. He said, "Fear was written on every man's face, as I knew it must have been on mine.

"First day we sang and listened to the distant sounds traveling through the rock, the sounds of the rescue party working their way toward us. Third day an extra heavy shot sent a concussion through the workings that put out our candles. All of our matches were water-soaked and useless.

"With the absolute darkness the sounds of our watches, all 20 of them, were as loud as a drum corps practice. After a few hours I crawled from man to man, collecting the watches and dropped them into a water-filled hole in the floor.

"We rationed the little bit of food we had. Water dripped on us. We were cold. My teeth chattered constantly and I was forced to tie a bandana around my head and chin. Finally, on what must have been about the ninth day, there came a sudden shriek, then unintelligible words, another shriek and the sounds of a man running, a body falling or hitting something, more running, and all the time the sounds grew dimmer and dimmer. Then silence. There was not one of us who did not know what had happened. One of the stiffs had come to his limit and his mind had snapped.

"There came a sudden rush of ice-cold air. A voice shouted, 'Cover your eyes! We're coming in with lights.' On the way to the hospital I asked one of the rescuers, 'How many did you save?' And he replied, 'All but one.'"

# THE MOTHER LODE

The spring of 1859 Henry Comstock, a former mountain man, his friend and partner Emanuel Penrod and two Irishmen, Patrick McLaughlin and Peter O'Riley discovered what became known as the Comstock Lode, recognized as the greatest single mineral strike in history. Nearly one-half billion dollars worth of gold and silver were mined here. But the discoverers profited very little from their fabulous find.

Patrick McLaughlin, sold his claim for a mere $3,500 and after the money was spent he cooked in a Virginia City eating establishment and died a pauper. Peter O'Riley, held out and was rewarded with $45,000 for his claim. But he did not live to enjoy it. Within a few days of receiving the windfall he began hearing voices and was committed to a private hospital for the insane where the strange voices haunted him until his dying day.

Emanuel Penrod sold his claims for $8,000 and faded into obscurity. Henry T.P. Comstock sold his interest for $11,000, invested the money in a supply store and was broke within a few months. He was reduced to wandering around the growing settlement proclaiming, "I still own the mother lode. I own this here town. It ought to be named after me." Eventually he drifted away and in 1870 he shot himself and was buried without a headstone in Bozeman, Montana.

# OLD MAN'S STORY

A young couple arrived at the home of Ed Prefontaine and the man politely introduced himself and his wife and asked, "Could we have a word with you?"

The couple was invited in and while Mrs. Prefontaine served fresh-brewed coffee the man explained that he and his wife worked as hospital attendants. He said, "An old man came under our care. Before he passed away he revealed his secret, saying that many years ago he and two companions intercepted the gold shipment from Jacksonville to San Francisco. They took the gold and came here, to an abandoned mine up the gulch. They got in an argument and the old man killed his two companions.

"After that he left the country. He must have been a hell-raiser because he killed another man, was arrested and served a long term in jail. He never returned for the gold but said he marked the spot by driving a metal saddle horn into a madrona tree."

Ed reacted enthusiastically, responding, "I remember seeing a saddle horn pounded into a tree." He led the way to where he though the tree was located but evidently the saddle horn had been overgrown by the tree. The buried gold was never found.

# EARLY WINTER

"If we keep goin', before the week's out we'll be eating a home-cooked meal and warming our bones in a hot bath. But if we stop we're good as dead," a miner named Galligar told his companions.

The seven men had tempted fate and delayed leaving the diggings in Salmon River country until it was nearly too late in the year. And now winter threatened to trap the men in the Blue Mountains. Snow floated through the dark green forest and the men took turns breaking trail over the summit and down the west side to the Columbia plateau where the cold wind howled.

Galligar possessed iron-willed determination and, mile after weary mile, he pushed on while his companions could not keep up and were scattered out behind him across the broad plain. Galligar was the first to reach the settlement of The Dalles.

A rescue party was quickly organized and within the first few miles two survivors were found. Of the remaining four men, two had severely frostbitten toes and fingers that had to be amputated. One frozen body was located. The last man was brought in alive, placed in a hotel bed where he shivered for two days and nights and died.

# RUMORS OF GOLD

Henry Hill listened to the rumors that gold had been discovered in California. He caught the gold fever and walked away from his Willamette Valley homestead, bought an Indian canoe and paddled to the mouth of the Columbia where he joined a group of other anxious men working to salvage a derelict, *The Starling*.

They re-floated the ship and made necessary repairs but *The Starling*, her timbers water-logged and leaking badly, was barely seaworthy. The greenhorn crew ignored the way the old ship wallowed crossing over the dangerous Columbia River bar and into the open ocean. They swung south, added all the sails they had and managed to keep the ship afloat long enough to reach San Francisco harbor where they abandoned her. They took passage on a small boat to Sacramento and walked the remaining miles to the mines at Hangtown.

Hill and three companions staked adjacent claims and worked them for a year and a half before the gold petered out. The largest nugget they found was worth $30 and twice they took out $400 of gold in a day. Hill headed north with $4,300 worth of gold in his poke.

During his absence a flood of settlers had reached the Willamette Valley and only a portion of his original homestead remained. But he used his grubstake earned in the California mines to buy back his land and eventually acquired over 1,000 acres of prime farmland.

# KILLED FOR GOLD

Thomas Moran was born in the state of New York. At the age of 24 he came west to strike it rich in the gold diggings in Idaho. He found a pocket of placer gold and worked it down to hardpan.

With the gold played out he strapped a money belt, with twenty pounds of gold, around his waist and set out horseback, riding to the west coast where he figured to catch passage on a ship that would return him to the east coast.

As Moran traveled he became aware of two men following him. He traveled faster and they traveled faster. He slowed and they slowed. Finally he came out of the timbered Blue Mounain and as he neared the Umatilla River the two men overtook him. He exchanged small talk with the strangers and they rode on.

Moran tried to laugh at what he figured was his over-active imagination. He was not being followed and yet he could not completely shake the uneasy feelings gnawing at him. That night he slept fitfully. At dawn he awoke to the sound of galloping horses. He jumped to his feet as the two men who had been following him rode into camp brandishing weapons.

Moran made a quick grab for his six-shooter. Shots were exchanged. One of the men fell, mortally wounded. Moran was shot in the chest and the remaining outlaw stripped him of the money belt.

"I was the one who found Moran," said Alfred Marshal, a local stockman. "Before he died Moran told me his story. His last words were, 'Bury me beside the Oregon Trail so I can watch the comin' and goin'.' That's exactly what I did."

To this day Thomas Moran lies in a grave on a hill east of Pendleton, Oregon, overlooking what was the Oregon Trail but today is Interstate 84.

# KLONDIKE GOLD

The summer of 1896 two white men and two Indians were prospecting on a tributary of the Yukon called Thron-Diuck by the natives. The white men had trouble pronouncing the word and simply called it Klondike. The men, Robert Henderson, a Canadian, George Carmack, an American who had come north and married Kate, an Indian woman, and Skookum Jim and Tagish Charlie began working a sandbar on Rabbit Creek, a tributary of the Klondike. The first pan produced a quarter ounce of gold and the stream was quickly renamed Bonanza Creek.

The four men mined a fortune in gold and when they came out George Carmack, his wife Kate, and Skookum Jim and Tagish Charlie, caught passage on a ship. Upon reaching Seattle they took rooms at the Seattle Hotel. Kate found the stairs and long corridors to be a confusing maze and blazed a trail from her room to the lobby by gouging chunks of wood from the doors and banisters with a knife.

Word of the big strike in the Klondike spread like wildfire and when other lucky miners arrived in Seattle from the rich diggings they too took rooms at downtown hotels and went on wild spending sprees. It was reported that one miner was lugging a suitcase so loaded with gold the handle broke. Another miner's wife, when she heard that her husband had brought out $112,000 of gold, promptly walked away from her job as a washerwoman, telling her customers, "Fish out your own clothes. I don't have to work no more and I ain't agonna."

# THE KLONDIKE DREAM

The discovery of gold in the Klondike launched the biggest, wildest and most futile gold rush in history.

After arriving on the Alaskan coast the Klondikers faced a 550-mile journey to the diggings. They were required to have a year's worth of supplies with them as well as working tools, cooking utensils, a tent, clothing, gun and ammunition, blankets and medicine. Most men packed one load a ways and returned for another, leapfrogging their supplies and gear over the pass to the head of the waterway. Those with money purchased pack animals. The winter of 1897-1898 it was estimated 3,000 horses perished and the route to Dawson City became known as Dead Horse Trail. Writer Jack London noted, "The horses died like mosquitoes in the first frost.... They were smashed to pieces against the boulders, snapped their legs in the crevices and broke their backs falling with packs."

The gold rush was slowed at Lake Bennett as men built boats and rafts. After crossing the lake the waterway became more dangerous as Miles Canyon, Squaw Rapids, White Horse Rapids and a series of other less dangerous rapids had to be navigated.

It was estimated that 100,000 people took part in the Klondike gold rush. Fewer than half ever reached the diggings and less than 4,000 miners were among the lucky few who actually found any gold.

# WHISPERS

The man, he said his name was Hughes, was on his deathbed and Officer C. H. Roth bent to hear the whispered last words of the old miner.

"We were way back in the mountains of Idaho," claimed Hughes. "Swan, he was my partner, we located a vein of ore so rich it was almost pure gold.

"Every year, after the snow was gone, we would pack in and worked that rich vein. Every fall we came out with bags of gold. It took us all winter to spend it. Lived high, we did."

Hughes expelled a long sigh, coughed a time or two and was quiet. The only sounds in the room were the ticking of a mantel clock and the labored breathing of the old man. Then he opened his eyes and began to whisper once again. "One year I took sick. Swan went in alone. On the way out, he was waylaid ... robbed ... murdered.

"Lot of years gone by since then. Don't know where all the time it went. Always thought I'd get over the sickness. Thought I'd work the mine again. Doesn't look like I ever will. Give me a piece of paper and a pencil. I'll draw a map. You can have the gold."

After the map was completed Roth examined it in detail. He started to ask the old man a question and realized Hughes was no longer in this world.

For twenty years Roth, a Spokane policeman, spent his vacations with the map, tramping around in the rugged Salmon River country. But he never found the entrance to the mine and the vein of gold.

24

# SONG OF THE FALLS

Tom Bell was a prospector who visited all the best diggings in the West. His constant companion was his fiddle and even though he was never one of the lucky few to strike it rich, he was a happy man. He had his music.

After his prospecting days were over Tom moved to the Snake River where he lived in a little cabin perched on a basalt ledge overlooking Shoshone Falls. He operated a small ferry above the falls.

One day three local men asked Tom to ferry them across the river. According to one of the men, "Old Tom took us across and then pushed off on his return leg. We sat on a rock and watched him. At mid-stream we were horrified to see the cable snap and the ferryboat spin out of control in the treacherous current above the falls.

"Old Tom jumped to his feet, tucked his fiddle under his chin and commenced to play a song he had composed titled 'Song of the Falls.' I had heard him play it a hundred times or more.

"He played with such force and passion, the music seeming to match the roar of the falls, the sounds of water surging around boulders, even the soft lapping of waves running up against the shore. The water and music blended together in a symphony that surged, seethed, churned and raged. Ahh, the energy, the vitality, the intensity of it all!

"At the very brink of the falls the ferry boat, with the old man still standing and playing his fiddle, teetered a moment and then it was gone. But for a long moment the music continued, floating through the deep canyon and echoing off the walls, and then there was nothing."

# BLACK HILLS GOLD

In 1868 the U.S. government signed a treaty with the Sioux nation. The Indians were to give up their warlike ways and agree to be confined on the Black Hills reservation. It was promised that no white man would be allowed to set foot on this land.

But soon Lt. Col. George Custer was ordered to make a reconnaissance of the Indian land. Knowing the Indians might react violently to this intrusion he commanded a strong force that included 951 soldiers, 3 Gatling guns, 110 wagons, 1,900 horses and mules, 61 Indian scouts and a 16-man band. Two experienced prospectors were among the entourage and they found what Custer described as "gold in paying quantities." When the news of their discovery was publicized it unleashed a gold rush to the Black Hills.

The army attempted to hold back the prospectors but it was as impossible as trying to hold back an incoming tide. The federal government, recognizing the potential for a dangerous situation attempted to purchase the Black Hills. But the Sioux refused to sell it and negotiations broke down.

Custer and the 7th U.S. Cavalry regiment were sent in to resolve the conflict but the Indians, fighting to preserve their lands and keep the white man out, attacked Custer and massacred his forces. In retaliation more troops were sent in, the Indians were subdued and prospectors swarmed into the Black Hills staking claims and extracting gold from the homeland of the Sioux nation.

# QUEEN OF THE COMSTOCK

Eilley Orrum was a superstitious girl who claimed she could look into a crystal ball, a "peepstone" she called it, and foresee the future. She predicted. "Someday I will be proclaimed as a queen."

But in 1859 the young woman was a long way from royalty. She was twice-married, twice-divorced, living near the undiscovered Comstock Lode of western Nevada and operating a boarding house for the miners.

One time a border could not pay his monthly bill and in exchange offered Eilley a 10-foot strip of his mining claim in Gold Canyon. She took it. Within a few days the miner struck a fabulously rich vein of gold. Eilley was soon making more than $1,000 a day. She used the money to have a mansion built for her on Washoe Meadow, adorning it with lace curtains costing $1,200 each and fancy mirrors imported from Venice.

Eilley soon became known as the "Queen of the Comstock" but within a few years the rich vein of ore played out and, with the easy money no longer rolling in, Eilley was forced to give up her mansion. She drifted to Reno and later San Francisco where she worked as a fortune-teller. The Queen of the Comstock spent her last days in abject poverty and died in San Francisco as a ward of the state.

# THE DREDGE

Placer gold was discovered on Swauk Creek, a tributary of the Yakima River in Central Washington in the late 1800s. Miners worked the gravel and took out several million dollars worth of gold.

In the early 1900s a gold prospecting company purchased the rights to many of the claims along the creek and brought in a dredge. It operated by digging up the ancient streambed, discarding the large rocks and sifting the sand and gravel over a sluice. The lighter material was washed away and the gold dust and small nuggets were saved. The dredge chewed up the willows and the grassy meadow that lined the meandering stream, leaving in its wake unsightly windrows of coarse gravel and rocks.

When Swauk Creek had been picked clean the company removed the dredge. All was quiet for several years and then one day the valley echoed to, "Look! Look what I found!"

The finder, looking through the tailings on Swauk Creek, proudly showed off a gold nugget weighing several pounds. The dredge had missed it for the simple reason that the nugget was too large to fit through the rotating screen and had been discarded as nothing more than worthless rock.

# BONANZA

Three Irishmen—Jim Doyle, Jim Burns and John Harnan —wandered into Cripple Creek, Colorado and chanced upon a pie-shaped, one-sixth-acre parcel of unclaimed land. With pick and shovel they went to work and soon discovered a rich vein of gold.

The partners kept their discovery secret, knowing if word leaked out the owners of the adjacent mines would file suit against them. Doyle shrewdly told his companions, "We'll build a cabin, have a trap door in the floor and work only at night, by candlelight. Any sign of trouble we play possum until the coast is clear. By the time the owners get wise we'll have enough money to fight 'em in court."

Eventually the mine owners learned of what they termed "the smuggling operation" and filed an avalanche of suits, subpoenas and injunctions. By then the Irishmen had amassed a legal fund of nearly $100,000. They used it not only to block the proceedings against them but to launch counter suits and through tricky legal maneuvering, they were able to attack weak points in their neighbors' claims and thereby acquire their land. The attorneys parlayed one-sixth of an acre into a total of 183 acres. Ultimately this land yielded a bonanza of gold worth $65 million.

# KLONDIKE FEVER

"Been a prospector all my life," reflected Frederick Parker. "But I homesteaded this one hundred and sixty acres and I'm gonna stay. It's mine to keep."

Mr. Failing, chairman of the Portland, Oregon water committee said, "Mr. Parker, I'm sure you realize we must purchase your property to ensure the City of Portland has an adequate supply of water for the future. Every man has a price. What is your price, Mr. Parker?"

"Five thousand bucks."

"That is ridiculous. Property within a mile of downtown does not approach that price," said Mr. Failing.

"Take it or leave it," challenged Parker. He watched Mr. Failing walk away and took a long look around at the tall timber surrounding his meadow, the barn, the shanty house, the orchard and meandering Bull Run River. He knew he would get his price. All he needed was patience. Like Mr. Failing said, the City had to have his land.

Parker never budged from his price. Then one day in 1897 Parker appeared in Chairman Failing's office. He claimed, "Remember I said I was a prospector at heart. Well, they found gold in the Klondike. I'm scraping together a grubstake. I'm willin' to sell."

"How much?" asked the chairman.

"What do you have in your pockets?"

The chairman emptied his pockets, counted the money and announced, "Seventy-five dollars and change."

"I'll take it," declared Parker and handed over the deed. He was off to the Klondike.

# BLUE BUCKET

"I have a clear recollection of the events that led to our discovery of gold," stated W.H. Herren. "It began the fall of 1845 when Stephen Meek met our wagon train at Fort Boise and claimed he knew a shortcut to the Willamette Valley. We paid him $5 a wagon to guide us through but soon regretted our decision. We became lost and roamed across the alkali flats and the forested hills without knowing where we were going.

"I remember that we left Malheur River and went up a rocky hollow and out onto and over a high ridge of mountains. From the mountains we descended to a creek, arriving late in the afternoon. We turned our stock loose to graze. My cousin, Dan Herren, and I went up the creek to check on the animals and after about two miles Dan found a peculiar yellow rock in some muddy cattle tracks. He slipped it into his trouser pocket. We found several more of the stones and saved these, too. We had read about gold dust but did not know that it existed in chunks. We never thought about it being gold."

"Twenty people died during our agonizing trip. It was not until the survivors reached the Willamette Valley that the yellow rocks were recognized as gold. Many from our group have attempted to retrace the wanderings of the wagons and locate the small creek where the gold was found. But to this day no one has discovered the source of what has become known as the Blue Bucket Mine."

# FEATHER MATTRESS

When gold was discovered in California in 1848 Tom and Martha Shadden talked it over and decided their future was not in sifting the gravel but in supplying the needs of the miners. Martha recalled, "We opened a little trading post along the Feather River. I planted a big garden, tended it dutifully and sold my produce for whatever the traffic would bear.

"I had made Tom promise that when we accumulated $50,000 in savings we would move to Oregon and buy a farm. I had heard such glowing reports about Oregon. We reached our goal, sold the trading post and loaded everything we owned in a wagon and started for San Francisco. The gold was secreted in a feather mattress.

"Upon reaching the bay we arranged passage on the sailing ship *Ajax*. The crew began loading our things. Some of the contents of the wagon were accidentally dropped in the water. One of those items was the feather mattress and even though it was laden with gold, the down feathers and air trapped inside kept it from sinking. It floated just below the surface and an outgoing tide was attempting to pull it into the bay.

"Tom shouted to a man operating a small rowboat, 'Fetch my feather mattress. I'll give you twenty dollars.'

"The boatman saved the mattress, collected his money and remarked, 'That's the heaviest and lumpiest feather mattress I ever thought of totin'.'"

# THE LONG WALK

The winter of 1859 Peter Mann was employed to carry 50 pounds of gold dust from Salem, Oregon to the mint in San Francisco. He took the stage south to the foothills of the Siskiyou Mountains where, because of deep snow, he was forced to shoulder a pack and set off on snowshoes.

Reaching the first way station along the trail, Mann was warned by the man living there, "Big storm comin' in. My knee always aches just before a big blow and its hurtin' somethin' fierce. If I was you, I'd stay put right here an' wait it out."

"Can't," claimed Mann. "Got to be going."

Mann departed, fully expecting to reach the next way station on schedule, but as predicted the storm hit the mountains and it snowed so hard he lost the trail. With dark descending he tried to start a fire but his matches were wet. He knew if he stopped walking he would freeze to death and throughout the long night he circled the trunk of a tree.

With morning light Mann started south on a route he hoped would take him out of the mountains. He walked all that day and again spent the night walking circles around a tree.

On the sixth day of his ordeal Mann arrived at a mining camp on Smith River. A friend of his said, "He came in dragging his pack and was so wore down that, at first, I couldn't figure out who he was."

Mann spent several weeks with his friend and then borrowed a horse and delivered the fifty pounds of gold to the mint in San Francisco.

# JACKASS

Noah Kellogg enjoyed spinning the yarn about the time his jackass made the "Big Strike" in the Coeur d'Alene district of northern Idaho. He claimed, "That jackass was always runnin' off. Spent more time lookin' for Jack than I ever did prospectin'. Well, this one time, in the middle of the night, Jack takes off. Come morning my partners and I went to trackin' him.

"Jack took the most difficult route he could, up and down hills and ravines and over windfalls. Finally we come out on this little bench and Jack was standing there, apparently mesmerized by some object. His ears were set forward, his eyes fixed and he was so totally absorbed. Then, to my utter amazement, I saw he was standin' on a great outcroppin' of silver and it was so bright it was reflectin' the sun's rays like a gigantic mirror. My partners and I wasted no time in filin' claims."

The ore that Jack found that day was galena, a mixture of lead and silver, and over the course of 60 years the Bunker Hill mine yielded $300 million. But Jack was never rewarded.

Instead, according to Noah, "That jackass run off one too many times so I strapped a stick of dynamite on his back, drove him down off a mountainside where even a goat could not keep its footin'. A few seconds later there was an explosion an' I fell on my knees and gave thanks 'cause never again would I have to chase that ornery jackass."

# LOST CABIN MINE

The fall of 1870 Constantine Magruder, a storekeeper and his physician friend, Dr. Lee, set up a hunting camp in the rugged Siskiyou Mountains. One day Magruder happened upon the remnants of an old log cabin. He investigated and found the roof caved in and trees growing through the hard-packed dirt floor. Evidently the cabin had been abandoned in a hurry because a chair was overturned, a plate and coffee cup remained on the table and there was a gold pan on the floor and the bottom of it was lined with gold nuggets. Magruder quickly collected the nuggets.

It was long after dark before Magruder made it back to camp. He told Dr. Lee about his discovery and produced the nuggets for proof.

"Think you can find that old cabin again?" asked Dr. Lee.

"Sure," replied his friend. They talked it over and decided to go to town in the morning, replenish their supplies and return to investigate the cabin and try to locate the gold diggings that, they figured, must be nearby.

After purchasing supplies the men headed back to the mountains but Magruder could not locate the cabin. An early snow forced them to retreat. They tried again in the spring and for years after but without success. To this day no one has found what has become known as the Lost Cabin Mine.

# THE CONFESSION

"Doc, any chance I'll pull through?" whispered the old man to the doctor of a small Nebraska town. The doctor looked very somber and shook his head.

"In that case I need to confess," the old man said. "This has been eating at me for better than thirty years. It happened way out in Idaho, as we were making our way to the mine. A mule freighter sold us a jug of whiskey. I had three partners. One was a rough customer, who claimed he had done a long stretch in the penitentiary.

"We drank on that jug and by the time we reached the trading post at Rock Springs the jug was gone and we were wanting more. I knew the owner of the trading post, Hugh Quinn. He was a good man, real quiet fellow, never carried a gun. When we asked him for a jug he said, 'Ain't got no liquor. Can't sell somethin' I don't got none of.'

"'You got a jug. Give it to me,' demanded my partner, the one who had done time in the penitentiary. He drew his pistol, pointed it at Quinn and pulled the trigger. That sobered me up in a big way. Sobered up the others, too. We talked about what to do and came up with a plan to make it look like a robbery. Then we rode away in a separate directions."

The old man closed his eyes. He said, "Dear God, I'm sorry for what I done. Don't punish me no more. Give me peace." And then he died.

# GRUBSTAKE

"Lucky Len was quite a character," claimed an acquaintance. "He was an old prospector and according to him he had been in on every major strike that was ever made. With his floppy brown hat, shaggy hair and untended beard he certainly did look the part. I do believe his last bath was one his mommy must have given him about a hundred years before.

"Lucky spent most of his time prospecting in the mountains. But every so often he led his mule into town and then Lucky liked to blow off a little steam. He drank to excess, but he was a likeable cuss and could sure enough talk a good story.

"If a greenhorn happened to be around, Lucky sidled up next to him and spun stories about fabulously rich ore veins and places where nuggets, big as a man's thumb, lay on top of the ground. He kept talking until the greenhorn finally caught gold fever and put up a grubstake. Then Lucky bought supplies and headed out, returning when he ran low on supplies.

"One greenhorn, who had grubstaked Lucky in the past, listened to Lucky's stories again and when he was asked for a grubstake he simply handed a cigar to the old prospector. When Lucky lit the cigar, which had been loaded with black powder, it exploded. From that day on Lucky was a bit more selective about who he asked for a grubstake."

# INDIAN SILVER

Prospector Sam Conger stumbled upon a camp of Arapahos and what intrigued him was that all the Indians wore shiny silver ornaments. He arranged a meeting with Chief Bird and asked him to share the secret of the source of the silver. Chief Bird refused.

Learning that the chief had a daughter, Mourning Dove, Sam decided to court her. He told her fantastic stories about life in the white man's world: railroads, ships with billowing sails, talking wire of the telegraph, great cities where women rode in carriages, wore flowing dresses and carried parasols to protect them from the weather. Sam promised, "Meet me tonight. Take me to the silver and I will marry you and show you the white man's world."

Mourning Dove made her way to the rendezvous but she was intercepted by her father and sent back to the tepee. Chief Bird continued to the meeting ground and reproached Sam, telling him the silver belonged to the Arapahos. "Look no more for it," he ordered.

In time the Arapaho were removed and placed on a distant reservation. Sam felt free to pursue his search and, using information given to him by Mourning Dove, he located a vein of exposed ore near the Continental Divide. In the ensuing years his mine, the Caribou, produced $8 million worth of silver.

# LAST WISH

Ed Schieffelin ran away from home at the age of 14 and headed for the gold diggings in the Salmon River country. But his parents intercepted him and brought him home. When Ed turned 17 he began his career as a prospector, traveling to California and on to Nevada, Utah, Colorado and finally to Arizona where the Apache Indians were on the warpath. For protection Ed fell in with a company of soldiers, making prospecting sorties on his own.

When Ed discovered an incredibly rich silver ledge he named it Tombstone because one of the soldiers had told him, "If you keep looking, what you are likely to find is your tombstone."

Ed became wealthy beyond comprehension. He bought a house in Los Angeles and tried to live the good life, but he was born to prospect. When gold was discovered in Alaska he took passage on a schooner and searched along the Yukon River but found very little gold. He returned to California where he married a society woman. But before long he left her and drifted north to Oregon and began prospecting.

The first week of May, 1897 he wrote a letter stating, "I have found stuff here that will make Tombstone look like salt. This is GOLD!"

Ten days later Ed was found dead beside a mortar and pestle where he had been grinding ore. The ore assayed $2,000 a ton. The source has never been located.

# TENDERFOOT

In 1905 speculators were elated when a tenderfoot prospector was said to have stumbled across a rich vein of gold in the Wallowa Mountains of Northeastern Oregon. A group of Easterners took control, forming the Tenderfoot Mining and Milling Company and selling stock for 15 cents a share.

A ten-mile road was built to the site and a sawmill, 20-stamp quartz mill and a cyanide plant were brought in on mule-drawn wagons. A boarding house and a bunkhouse were built and work began on a residence for the mine superintendent.

The president of Merchants National Bank in Portland visited the mine and claimed the Tenderfoot would rival the strikes in Cripple Creek, Tonapah and the Klondike. The announcement sent the stock, which had been trading at 65 cents, skyrocketing. Everything was rosy until tests showed only the face rock held any value. According to one report, "It was clear that someone had loaded a shotgun shell with gold and fired it into the rock."

The Tenderfoot Mine folded. Over the years souvenir hunters have hauled off most of the machinery and the buildings have yielded to the weather. All that remains of the Tenderfoot Mining and Milling Company is a shallow hole in the ground and a pile of worthless stock.

# TWO-FRENCHMEN MINE

The summer of 1863 two Frenchmen discovered a rich gold deposit in the Cascade mountains of Oregon. That fall they came out of the mountains and exchanged their bulky gold for currency. They took passage on a ship bound for San Francisco and passed the winter there living an extravagant lifestyle. When they had spent all their money they headed north to Oregon to collect more gold.

On the way to the mine they captured an Indian woman and held her as their slave. It was several months before she could escape and return to her people. The woman's brother swore vengeance and, along with a party of warriors, he located the Frenchmen's cabin and killed both of the miners.

White settlers to the Klamath basin heard the story of the Two-Frenchmen Mine and the fabulously rich strike they had made. Many attempts were made to persuade the Indians to lead the way to the cabin but they always refused. The brother outlived his sister and all the warriors who had been involved in the attack on the miners. Just before he died in 1924 he was asked to reveal the location of Two-Frenchmen Mine. He refused.

# HIGH BIDDER

"What advice would I give to a woman about to go to the Klondike? Stay away. It is no place for a woman," advised Mrs. Clancy Berry after her arrival in Dawson City the fall of 1896.

But women continued to follow the prospectors to the Klondike. One of the most talked about was a young French-Canadian named Mabel LaRose. She worked in the Monte Carlo Dance Hall and Saloon in Dawson City. According to her, "I'm not like some of the other girls. I live private."

Her professional status changed the night she requested one of the miners to boost her up on the bar. For a long moment she stood looking over the smoky sea of faces. The piano player abruptly stopped playing. Voices died away. A hush fell over the room. Miss LaRose called out, "Boys, I'm for sale. Highest bidder takes all. I'll serve as your wife, wife in every respect of the word."

The boys knew exactly what she meant and roared their approval. "Five hundred bucks," came the first bid and this set off a spirited round of bidding that eventually reached $5,000. The crowd hooted and cheered as Miss LaRose and her "husband" walked arm-in-arm through the swinging doors and into the night.

# CACHE OF GOLD

Levi MacGruder was a trader who traveled to the mining camps of Idaho and Montana swapping food and supplies for gold. On August 3, 1863 he departed Lewiston, Idaho with a hundred-mule pack train.

The first of October a friend, Hill Beachy, received a letter from MacGruder stating the trader was headed home with $30,000 in gold dust and another $20,000 in gold coin. Near the middle of the month a man arrived in town riding MacGruder's distinctive paint horse. Beachy confronted the man and learned the names of the four men who had sold him the horse - William Page, S.C. Lowry, David Howard and James Romaine.

Beachy trailed the men to San Francisco where he found William Page registered as a guest in a small hotel on California Street. Page quickly confessed and with his help the other men were arrested. At the trial, held in Lewiston, Page testified he had been forced to participate and that Howard, Lowry and Romaine had killed MacGruder and pushed his body off a high cliff. Fearing the gold coins would tie them to the crime, they had buried them at the base of this cliff.

The three guilty men were hanged on March 4, 1864. Page was set free and although he made several attempts to locate the cache of gold coins he was never able to locate the cliff. Within a few months he died. To this day the gold remains buried along the old freight trail about a day's ride east of Walla Walla, Washington.

# WIND RIVER RAVING

A gaunt man, his clothes in shreds and staggering on frostbitten feet, arrived at a prospector's camp. He raved about gold and an Indian attack. Piecing together his story it appeared the delirious man, along with two partners, had been prospecting in the Wind River Range and, after finding nuggets in a creek, they had located an exposed gold vein on a canyon wall.

One evening, when his partners did not return from working the mine, the man had gone in search of them and found blood on the rocks at the entrance to the mine.

The deranged man suddenly stopped his ramblings, cocked his head and said, "Did you hear that? Gunshots." He ducked his head under his blanket and it was a long time before he cautiously peeked out and resumed his strange discourse, "Play dead. Don't move. Here they come. Indians!"

The man, who later gave his name as Hurlburt, recovered and when he was once again rational he told how he had made his way out of the mountains after the Indian attack, how he had been trapped in a blizzard and been forced to exist on the bark he stripped off trees and ate. Once he killed a porcupine and carried the carcass with him, feeding on it, for days.

Hurlburt enlisted the support of a number of the miners, and led several expeditions, but he was never able to locate the lost mine of the Wind River Range.

# CHANCE ENCOUNTER

"The spring of 1862 I set out for Eastern Oregon, where gold had recently been discovered," related Thomas Brents. "Upon reaching the diggings I learned all the good claims had been filed on and decided my best opportunity was to establish an express service between the mines and the nearest settlement in The Dalles.

"Transporting gold out and bringing in supplies proved quite a successful enterprise for me. On one of my trips I reached the Deschutes River at dark and saw a cheery campfire blazing on the far side. After swimming the swollen stream a warm meal, and company for the evening, seemed mighty appealing to me.

"I called a hello and asked if I could come in. A reassuring voice welcomed me. But when I saw the man who had spoken, I became extremely nervous because I recognized the face from wanted posters. It was the outlaw Berry Way and he was camped with his gang of cutthroats, some of whom I also recognized.

"I pulled my saddle and unloaded my pack string. When I removed the express sack one of the gang demanded to know what was in the sack. I assured him, 'No treasure here. Just mule shoes for a pack train coming upriver.' I nonchalantly threw the sack on the ground and never touched it again. I spent a sleepless night and in the morning continued on my way.

"A few days after my chance encounter, the vigilantes caught Berry Way. They hung him from a tree limb."

# MIRACLE MINER

In 1914 Dick Roelofs was the mining engineer in charge of operating the Cresson Mine at Cripple Creek, Colorado. One day, while he was checking on a crew at the 1,200 foot level, the miners broke through a wall to expose a cavity. Roelofs stepped forward to have a look.

He gave a sharp whistle at what his miner's light revealed. The cavity was ablaze with gleaming gold-laced quartz hanging from the ceiling and clinging to the walls. The floor was littered with gold nuggets and shimmering white quartz.

"This is it! Boys, you've hit the big one," Roelofs told the men. An ironworker was brought in and a door was installed to block access to the vault. The absentee owners were notified and quickly gave the order, "Clean it out."

Roelofs selected his most trusted miners and they scraped the walls of the cavity, which measured 20 feet long, 15 feet wide and 40 feet high, and filled 1,400 sacks with crystals and gold. The payout was worth more than a million dollars.

Dick Roelofs, who became known as the "Miracle Miner," was given a substantial reward for the find. He quit the mine, moved to New York and spent the remainder of his days enjoying the good life.

# THE STRIKE

Henry Griffin and his partner, David Littlefield, had searched for the fabled Blue Bucket Mine, wandering across the High Desert for a number of weeks. They had grown discouraged and were ready to give up and return home. But one evening Griffin hiked up a small creek and tried his hand at prospecting. He shoveled gravel into his pan, washed it and when he looked the bottom of the pan showed flecks of color.

"Gold! I found gold!" he shouted. Littlefield rushed to his side and stood staring at the dull yellow residue in the pan. Griffin's discovery, on October 23, 1861, was the first gold strike located in Eastern Oregon. Prospectors rushed to the site and within a few short months the town of Auburn boasted a population of more than 5,000. The wide-open town became the center of a mining district and attracted not only the miners but also a host of gamblers and questionable characters. When the gold began to play out the Chinese moved in to gather the last traces of the precious metal.

The town of Auburn disappeared. All that endures are three cemeteries, two for Chinese and a one where several white men, including Henry Griffin, are buried.

# THE CHINESE

In the Old West the Chinese were despised and hated because of their race and the fact they were willing to work for wages so low they undercut the pay of Americans. In Virginia City, Nevada 1,500 Chinese were chased into the hills and held there until they agreed not to work in the mines. At Rock Springs, Wyoming 28 Chinese were killed in a race riot. Throughout the West the Chinese were discriminated against, harassed and killed. They were forced to rework old diggings from which most of the gold had already been extracted. But they lived frugally and were industrious and often managed to accumulate large sums of gold.

Chinese miners came to the Snake River canyon in the 1860s, working their way upriver from Lewiston, pulling boats loaded with supplies and prospecting as they traveled. When they located a placer pocket they built dugouts and walled the fronts with stone. Usually one dugout was used as a cookhouse and storeroom and another for living quarters.

In 1887 a congregation of Chinese miners were camped where Big Deep Creek empties into the Snake River. They were attacked and massacred by a band of renegade white men. It was a stern warning to all other Chinese in the area and they hastily departed, leaving behind supplies and, in some instances, even their gold.

# IRON BOX

Skeedaddle Smith lived his last few years up Birch Creek in Northeast Oregon. The rumor was that the old miner had buried his gold, more than 40 pounds, somewhere near his cabin. His death set off a round of treasure hunting fever.

In 1906, more than 40 years after the old man died, a storekeeper named J. H. Anderson received a tip concerning Skeedaddle's gold. He rode horseback to the town of Pilot Rock and asked at the mercantile store for directions to the old Skeedaddle Smith place.

He was told, "Go down Birch Creek 'til you come to the emigrant trail. His ol' house and the outbuildings burned years ago but just ask any of the neighbors, they can tell ya where it was."

"Thanks a lot," replied Anderson. He rode away. That evening he returned to town and was eating supper at the local café when several men approached his table. One of the men said, "You visited Skeedaddle Smith's old place today, dug two dry holes but the third ya hit somethin' didn't ya? What was in that iron box?"

"Boys, I don't know what you're on earth you're talking about," claimed Anderson, dabbing at the corner of his mouth with a handkerchief. He shoved his chair away from the table and stood. "If you'll excuse me I have to be going." He paid for his meal and rode out of town. No one ever knew if he found the gold, but rumor had it that he did.

# THE GOLD SHIPMENT

"This is a hold-up," barked the highwayman as he stepped from behind a boulder and leveled his rifle at the stage driver. "Throw down the Wells Fargo box."

The driver tied the lines to the brake lever and struggled with the strongbox. After it dropped to the ground he was ordered down and was bound and gagged. He watched as the holdup man broke open the express box with a miner's pick, scoop up greenbacks, gold coins and sacks of gold, loaded the treasures onto a packhorse and departed into the growing darkness.

The thief headed west and climbed into the Cascade Mountains where he buried the gold, built a log cabin and lived the life of a hermit. He remained here for eight long years before he ventured out of the mountains and discovered another man had been convicted of his crime and was serving time at the Idaho State Penitentiary. Upon hearing this news he felt such a stab of remorse that he suffered a heart attack.

On his deathbed he confessed to stealing the Wells Fargo gold shipment and gave precise directions from his cabin to the stump where he had buried the greenbacks and nearly 100 pounds of gold. But he died before he could give directions to his Cascade mountain cabin.

# DELIVERING MAIL

J.M. Shepherd was an enterprising young man who started a mail delivery service between Walla Walla, Washington and the diggings along the Snake and Salmon rivers in Idaho.

One day, on Shepherd's way back from the Snake River mines, he noticed an approaching rider. As the stranger drew near he recognized the man from a wanted posters as the notorious outlaw French Charley. Reining in Shepherd braced himself for trouble.

French Charley rode up and demanded to know, "You coming from the mines?"

"Yep," Shepherd told him.

"Carrying gold?"

"Yep."

"How much?"

Shepherd answered truthfully, "About 70 pounds. Are you gonna rob me."

"You needn't fear me," stated French Charley. "I don't rob from the working man, only from rich companies that can afford to lose a little now and then. But a word of warning—these hills are full of bandits who are not so discriminating as me. If you happen to run into any of them and they give you trouble, just tell them French Charley says to leave you alone. You've got safe passage."

# THE LAST HOLDUP

The evening of December 5, 1916 was bitter cold and when the stage did not arrive as scheduled in Jarbridge, Nevada a search party was organized. They found the stage only a mile from town. The horses had been tied to a limb in a grove of trees, the brakes were frozen to the rim of the wheels, and slumped across the seat was the body of the driver, riddled with bullet holes. The payroll box with $40,000 was missing.

"Look at this!" called one of the investigators and he pointed out the tracks of a man and a dog. The first name to come up as a possible suspect was Ben Kuhl, a man who lived only a few miles from the scene of the crime. Kuhl was a surly recluse whose only companion was a yellow mongrel. The dog was lured from Kuhl's cabin and led to the grove where it was discovered its paw prints perfectly matched the tracks left in the snow the night before.

Kuhl was arrested and charged with murder. But he denied any knowledge of the crime. He stood trial, was found guilty of first-degree murder and served 27 years in the Nevada State Prison. Three days after his release, as he was walking along the road toward Jarbridge, he was struck and killed by an automobile.

Ben Kuhl became a unique footnote in western history— as the last man convicted of robbing a stage.

# THE MATCHLESS

Horace Tabor was born in Vermont, learned the stonecutter trade and married Augusta Pierce. They came west to seek their fortune in the gold fields. Eventually Horace gave up prospecting and opened a general store.

One day two prospectors asked Horace for a grubstake. He gave them $17 worth of supplies in return for one-third of their earnings. The men discovered an outcropping of silver and Horace sold his interest for a million dollars and began living the high life. He divorced Augusta, his wife of 25 years, and married a young woman, a beautiful divorcee named Baby Doe. A Denver newspaper described her as, "tall and well-proportioned, with a complexion so clear it reminds one of the blush of a rose mingling with pure white lily."

Horace bought his bride a $7,000 wedding dress and a $90,000 diamond necklace; lavishing gifts on her at the same time the financial panic of 1893 was cleaning out his bank account. Creditors took everything, including the mansion, property holdings and even Baby Doe's jewelry.

Horace died in a rundown Denver hotel. Baby Doe lived another 36 years and continued to cling to the hope that the Matchless Mine, the only property Horace had been able to keep, would make her rich again. But it never did. Her body was found in a dilapidated tool shed at the abandoned mine in 1935.

# GOLD RUSH AFTERMATH

The two men most responsible for the California gold rush were John Sutter and James Marshall. After Marshall discovered gold on the American River, 40 miles northeast of Sutter's Fort, the men working for Sutter deserted him and took up mining. The shops and the gristmills fell silent, hides rotted in the tanning vats and the crops spoiled in the fields.

Miners swarmed over Sutter's land and challenged his title to the property in court. Sutter finally gave up the sprawling land grant and moved to Pennsylvania. He died in 1880 while visiting Capitol Hill in an attempt to enlist Congress's help in winning compensation for his claims.

James Marshall also suffered a miserable fate. He joined in the search for gold but was luckless and never became wealthy. As his frustration mounted he boasted he was the rightful owner of all the gold in California. Miners drove him from one camp to the next. He finally took up residence in a small cabin on the American River, near where he had made the original discovery, living in abject poverty, a forgotten man, until death took him in 1885. Five years later the California legislature spent $9,000 on a statue in his likeness pointing at the exact spot where he had found the first nugget.

Rick Steber's Tales of the Wild West series feature
illustrations by Don Gray. The AudioBooks are narrated
by Dallas McKennon. Current titles in the series include:

**Other books written by Rick Steber—**

**www.ricksteber.com**

**Bonanza Publishing**
Box 204
Prineville, Oregon 97754